TALES OF GREAT GODDESSES

ATHENA

GODDESS OF WISDOM AND WAR

LIBRARY OF CONGRESS CONTROL NUMBER 2020947060

ISBN 978-1-4197-4859-2

ABRAMS The Art of Books
195 Broadway, New York, NY 10007
abramsbooks.com

GREAT GODDESSES

ATHENA

GODDESS OF WISDOM AND WAR

IMOGEN AND ISABEL GREENBERG

AMULET BOOKS • NEW YORK

FOR FRIEDA

WELCOME TO MOUNT OLYMPUS!

HERE THE GREEK GODS AND GODDESSES LIVED AS ONE BIG FAMILY, LAUGHING, PLAYING, SCHEMING, AND FIGHTING. FROM UP ON THE MOUNTAIN, THEY WATCHED OVER THE PEOPLE BELOW, WHO THEY CALLED MORTALS, HELPING OUT THEIR FAVORITES. BUT THEY ALSO LIKED TO MEDDLE IN THE LIVES OF THE OTHER GODS' AND GODDESSES' CHOSEN HEROES. THIS IS THE STORY OF THE GODDESS ATHENA, WHO WAS BRAVE, WISE, AND LOVED ADVENTURE. READ ON TO DISCOVER THE DARING TALES OF ATHENA, AND THOSE WHO CROSSED HER PATH!

1

IN THIS BOOK YOU WILL MEET

GODS AND GODDESSES

ATHENA

YOUNG AND BRAVE, ATHENA WAS

THE GODDESS OF WISDOM. SHE WAS KNOWN

FOR HELPING MORTALS, HEROES, AND DEMIGODS

ON THEIR ADVENTURES—BUT SHE OFTEN GOT

HERSELF INTO TROUBLE ALONG THE WAY!

ZEUS

ZEUS WAS KING OF ALL THE GODS,

AND HE LOVED HIS YOUNGEST DAUGHTER, ATHENA.

BUT HE ALSO HAD A TERRIBLE TEMPER.

HERA

HERA WAS THE WIFE OF ZEUS AND THE
OLDEST AND WISEST OF ALL THE GODDESSES.
SHE ALWAYS HAD A WORD OF ADVICE FOR ANY
YOUNG GODDESS IN NEED, ESPECIALLY
HER STEPDAUGHTER ATHENA.

APHRODITE

ATHENA'S SISTER

APHRODITE WAS THE GODDESS OF BEAUTY

AND FERTILITY. BUT ATHENA AND APHRODITE

DIDN'T ALWAYS GET ALONG.

POSEIDON

POSEIDON WAS ZEUS'S
BROTHER AND THE GOD OF THE SEAS.
HE WAS OLD, ARGUMENTATIVE, AND LIKED
THINGS HIS OWN WAY.

HEPHAESTUS

ZEUS'S SON AND ATHENA'S

HALF BROTHER, HEPHAESTUS WAS THE BLACKSMITH

OF THE GODS. HE COULD BE A LOT OF FUN,

BUT HE WAS ALSO FOOLISH.

HERMES

CLEVER AND MISCHIEVOUS,

HERMES IS THE GOD OF TRADE AND TRAVELERS.

HE'S A BIT OF A TRICKSTER, BUT HE CAN FLY

TO THE RESCUE IN A PINCH.

ARACHNE

ARACHNE CHALLENGED ATHENA TO
A WEAVING CONTEST. SHE WAS A TALENTED
AND AMBITIOUS MORTAL, BUT SHE LEARNED
THE HARD WAY THAT GETTING ON THE WRONG
SIDE OF THE GODS COULD BE DANGEROUS.

ERICHTHONIUS

ERICHTHONIUS WAS A DEMIGOD
AND THE SON OF HEPHAESTUS. ATHENA RAISED
HIM AS A BABY, BEFORE HE WAS ADOPTED BY A
YOUNG COUPLE IN ATHENS, WHERE HE
LATER BECAME KING.

PERSEUS

PERSEUS WAS A DEMIGOD
AND SON OF ZEUS, WHO LIVED AMONG THE
MORTALS. HE WAS CHALLENGED TO KILL MEDUSA,
AND ASKED FOR ATHENA'S HELP.

MEDUSA

MEDUSA WAS A GORGON WHO HAD
SNAKES GROWING OUT OF HER HEAD. STRONG
AND FEARSOME, ANYONE WHO LOOKED IN HER
EYES WOULD BE TURNED TO STONE.

ACHILLES

ACHILLES WAS THE GREAT

WARRIOR OF THE GREEKS IN THE TROJAN WAR.

HE WAS ALMOST UNSTOPPABLE IN BATTLE—

BUT ALSO QUITE VAIN.

ODYSSEUS

A CLEVER WARRIOR, ODYSSEUS
WON THE TROJAN WAR FOR THE GREEKS.
HE WAS BRAVE, BUT HIS SHIP WAS LOST IN A
STORM ON THE WAY HOME, AND HE WAS
STUCK AT SEA FOR TEN YEARS.

PARIS

PARIS WAS THE COWARDLY SON
OF KING PRIAM OF TROY. HE CAUSED
THE EPIC TROJAN WAR WHEN HE FELL IN LOVE
WITH HELEN, THE MOST BEAUTIFUL
WOMAN IN THE WORLD.

PART I

A Goddess Is Born

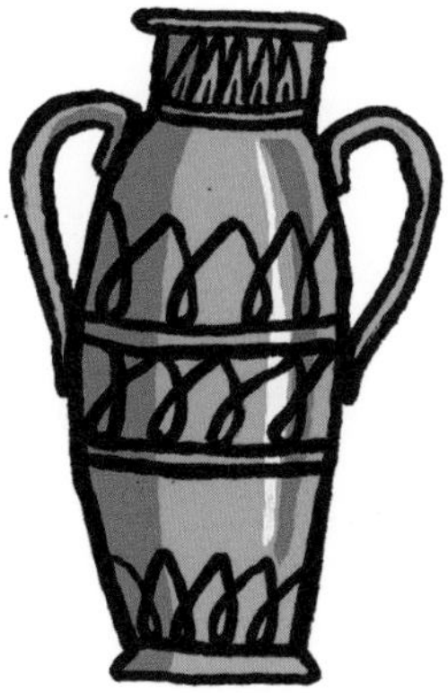

ONCE UPON A TIME ON MOUNT OLYMPUS, THE MIGHTY ZEUS—KING OF ALL THE GODS AND GODDESSES—HAD AN ALMIGHTY HEADACHE.

HE HAD JUST CREATED THE ENTIRE WORLD, BUT SOON AFTER, HE KNEW THAT THERE WAS SOMETHING MISSING. WHILE HE WAS THINKING ABOUT WHAT HE COULD HAVE FORGOTTEN, A HEADACHE APPEARED FROM NOWHERE, JUST LIKE THE WORLD HE HAD CREATED.

THE HEADACHE GREW AND RAGED. FOR DAYS, HE THUNDERED THROUGH THE WORLD, AND THE GROUND SHOOK AND THE SEAS SPUN IN GREAT WHIRLPOOLS, AND THE CLOUDS GATHERED LOWER, DARKER, AND HEAVIER EACH DAY. HIS SCREAMS OF PAIN ECHOED AROUND THE WORLD, AND ALL WAS DARKNESS AND MISERY.

BUT STILL HE COULDN'T
SHAKE THE HEADACHE.

ZEUS CALLED HIS SON HEPHAESTUS, THE BLACKSMITH OF THE GODS, TO BRING HIM THE STRONGEST HAMMER HE OWNED. WHEN HEPHAESTUS ARRIVED AT ZEUS'S THRONE ON THE HIGHEST PEAK OF OLYMPUS, ZEUS GAVE HIS ORDERS.

HEPHAESTUS DIDN'T KNOW WHAT TO DO. HURTING ZEUS WAS THE WORST THING A YOUNG GOD COULD DO—BUT REFUSING AN ORDER FROM HIM MIGHT BE JUST AS BAD.

HEPHAESTUS RAISED THE GIANT HAMMER. HE BROUGHT IT DOWN ON ZEUS'S HEAD WITH AN ECHOING CRASH. ZEUS LET OUT A ROAR OF PAIN AS HIS HEAD SPLIT OPEN, AND ATHENA JUMPED OUT! SHE WAS BORN DRESSED IN SHINING ARMOR, READY TO DO BATTLE. HER LIFE ON MOUNT OLYMPUS, HOME OF THE GREEK GODS AND GODDESSES, HAD BEGUN.

AT FIRST, THE OTHER GODS AND GODDESSES WERE SUSPICIOUS OF ATHENA. SHE WAS NEW, SHE WAS LOUD, AND SHE HAD CAUSED CHAOS WHEN SHE WAS BORN. ATHENA WOULD SOON LEARN THAT DOING THINGS IN A NEW WAY COULD MAKE THE OLD GODS VERY ANGRY.

ATHENA WAS GREETING HER BROTHERS AND SISTERS WHEN SHE HEARD A LOUD CHEER ECHO AROUND MOUNT OLYMPUS. THE CHEER STARTLED THE GODS AND GODDESSES, AND THEY RUSHED TO THE ROCK POOLS, MIRRORS, AND CLOUDS, WHICH WERE WINDOWS THAT LOOKED DOWN TO EARTH.

MANY, MANY MILES BELOW, IN THE OPEN PLAINS OF GREECE, HUNDREDS OF PEOPLE HAD JOINED TOGETHER. A CITY WAS BORN, AND THE RESIDENTS WERE ASKING FOR A GOD OR GODDESS TO LOOK AFTER THEM.

POSEIDON PUSHED HIS WAY THROUGH THE CROWD AND BOASTED, "OUT OF MY WAY! I'LL SPONSOR THIS NEW CITY AND THEY WILL NAME IT AFTER ME, THE GREATEST AND NOBLEST GOD."
A FEW OF THE GODS AND GODDESSES LOOKED DISAPPOINTED, BUT THEY DIDN'T DARE ARGUE WITH POSEIDON. HE WAS ZEUS'S BROTHER AND ONE OF THE OLDEST—AND ANGRIEST—GODS. HE CONTROLLED THE SEA, AND THIS CITY WAS NEAR THE COAST.

ATHENA DIDN'T LIKE THIS. SO SHE CONFRONTED HIM, "UNCLE POSEIDON, I WANT TO SPONSOR THE NEW CITY INSTEAD OF YOU." POSEIDON SPUN AROUND TO SEE WHO HAD SPOKEN, AND WHEN HE SAW IT WAS ATHENA, HE SHOUTED, "WHAT?! WHO IS THIS FOOLISH CHILD?" HE SWUNG HIS TRIDENT AROUND HIS HEAD AND ROARED AT HER. BUT ATHENA WASN'T SCARED AT ALL. POSEIDON WAS FURIOUS.

BUT ZEUS LOVED HIS DAUGHTER, AND HAD GROWN TIRED OF HIS BROTHER'S TANTRUMS.

POSEIDON COULDN'T BELIEVE IT—HOW DARE HIS OWN BROTHER ASK HIM TO COMPETE? HE GLARED AT ATHENA, WHO COULD BARELY CONTAIN HER EXCITEMENT.

23

THEY BOTH APPEARED BEFORE THE PEOPLE OF THE CITY, TO SHOW THEM WHAT THEY COULD DO IF THEY WERE CHOSEN AS THE PATRON GOD. ATHENA SPOKE FIRST: "I HAVE PLANTED AN OLIVE TREE. ITS FRUIT WILL KEEP THE PEOPLE OF THIS CITY WELL FED, AND YOU CAN TRADE IT FOR MILES AROUND. THESE WILL BE THE BEST OLIVES IN ALL OF GREECE!" THE PEOPLE NODDED THEIR APPROVAL. IT WAS A VERY GOOD GIFT—BEAUTIFUL AND PRACTICAL!

BUT POSEIDON WAS NOT IMPRESSED. "THAT'S THE WORST GIFT EVER," HE SNORTED. HE STOOD PROUDLY AT HIS FULL HEIGHT AND CRIED:

PEOPLE OF THIS CITY—
I WILL GIVE YOU WATER!

HE RAISED HIS TRIDENT OVER HIS HEAD
AND SPLIT A MIGHTY ROCK IN TWO. A STREAM APPEARED
AND WATER RUSHED THROUGH THE VALLEY. THE PEOPLE RAN FORWARD,
CUPPING THEIR HANDS TO TASTE THE WATER. POSEIDON CHUCKLED,
SURE THAT HE HAD BEATEN ATHENA. HE WAS ALREADY PLANNING
WHERE HIS TEMPLE WOULD BE. BUT ALL OF A SUDDEN, THE PEOPLE
SPAT THE WATER OUT. POSEIDON WAS THE GOD OF THE SEA, AND
THE WATER HE HAD BROUGHT WAS FAR TOO SALTY TO DRINK.
THE PEOPLE OF THE NEW CITY HAD DECIDED,
AND TOGETHER THEY CHORUSED:

We choose Athena!

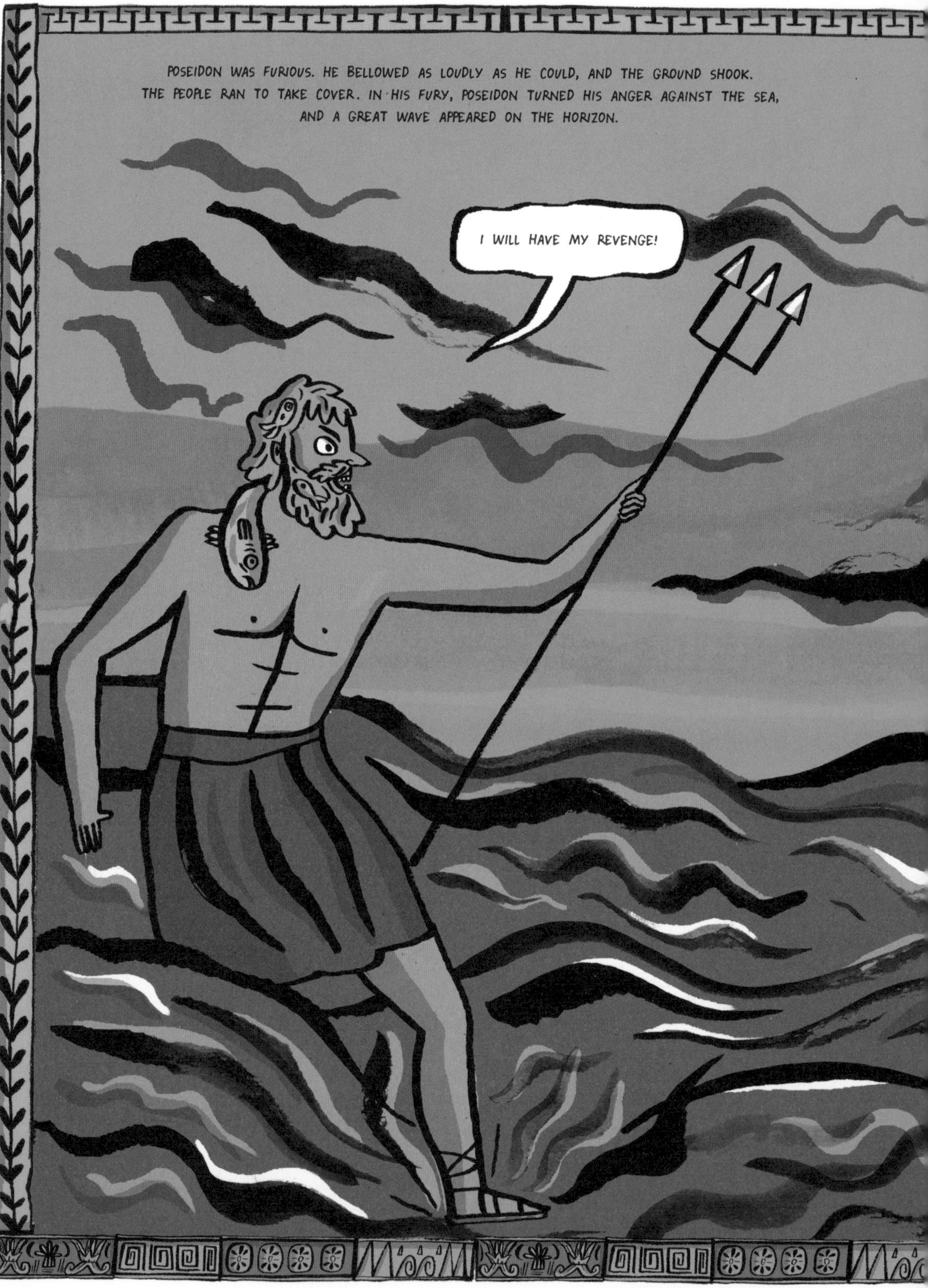
POSEIDON WAS FURIOUS. HE BELLOWED AS LOUDLY AS HE COULD, AND THE GROUND SHOOK. THE PEOPLE RAN TO TAKE COVER. IN HIS FURY, POSEIDON TURNED HIS ANGER AGAINST THE SEA, AND A GREAT WAVE APPEARED ON THE HORIZON.
I WILL HAVE MY REVENGE!

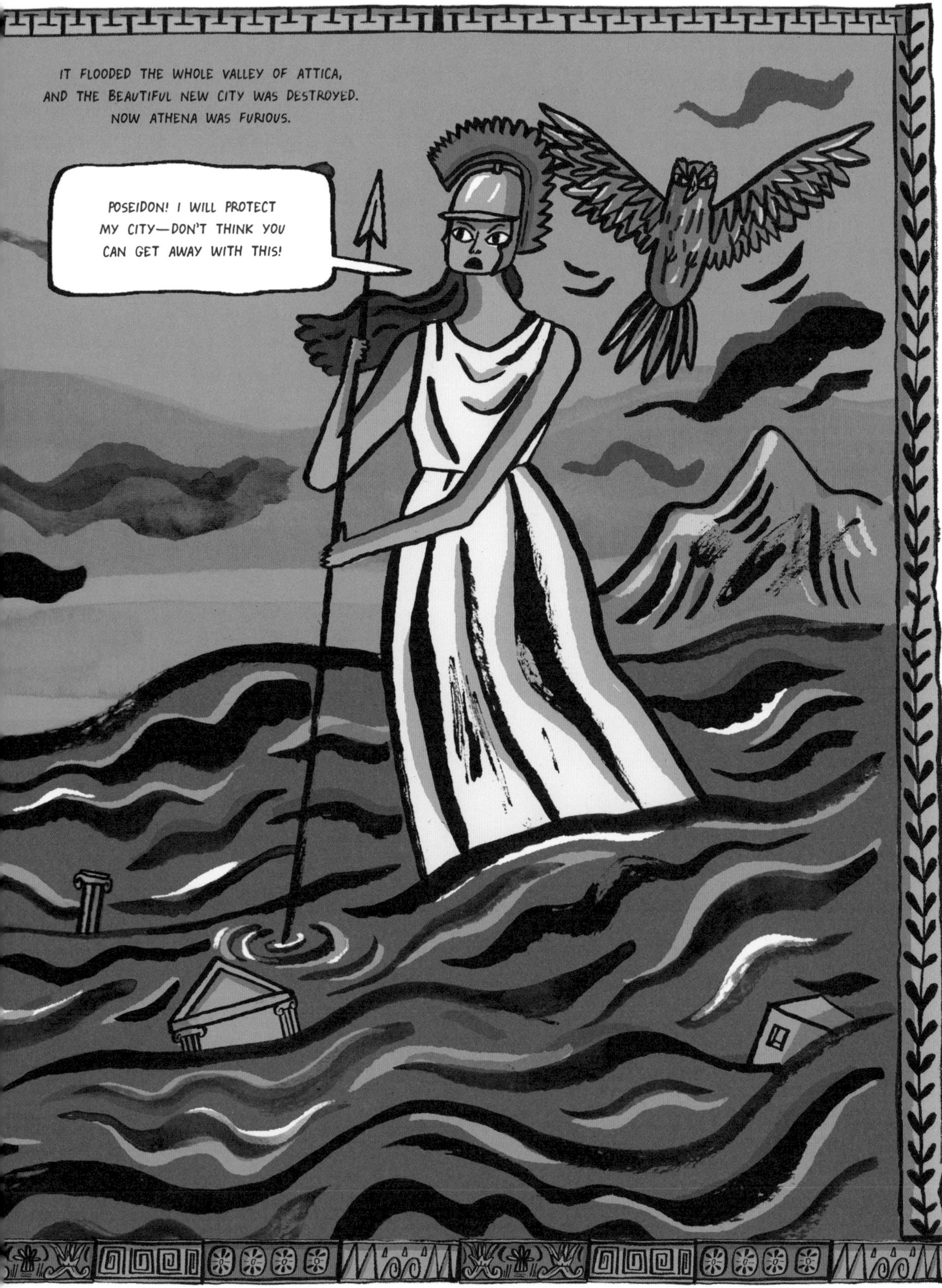
IT FLOODED THE WHOLE VALLEY OF ATTICA, AND THE BEAUTIFUL NEW CITY WAS DESTROYED. NOW ATHENA WAS FURIOUS.
POSEIDON! I WILL PROTECT MY CITY—DON'T THINK YOU CAN GET AWAY WITH THIS!

OVER TIME, THE PEOPLE REBUILT THEIR CITY, WITH ATHENA'S HELP. SHE LOVED HER NEW CITY, AND HER PEOPLE NAMED IT ATHENS, AFTER HER. THIS SMALL TOWN IN ATTICA SOON BECAME THE MOST POWERFUL CITY IN ALL OF ANCIENT GREECE.

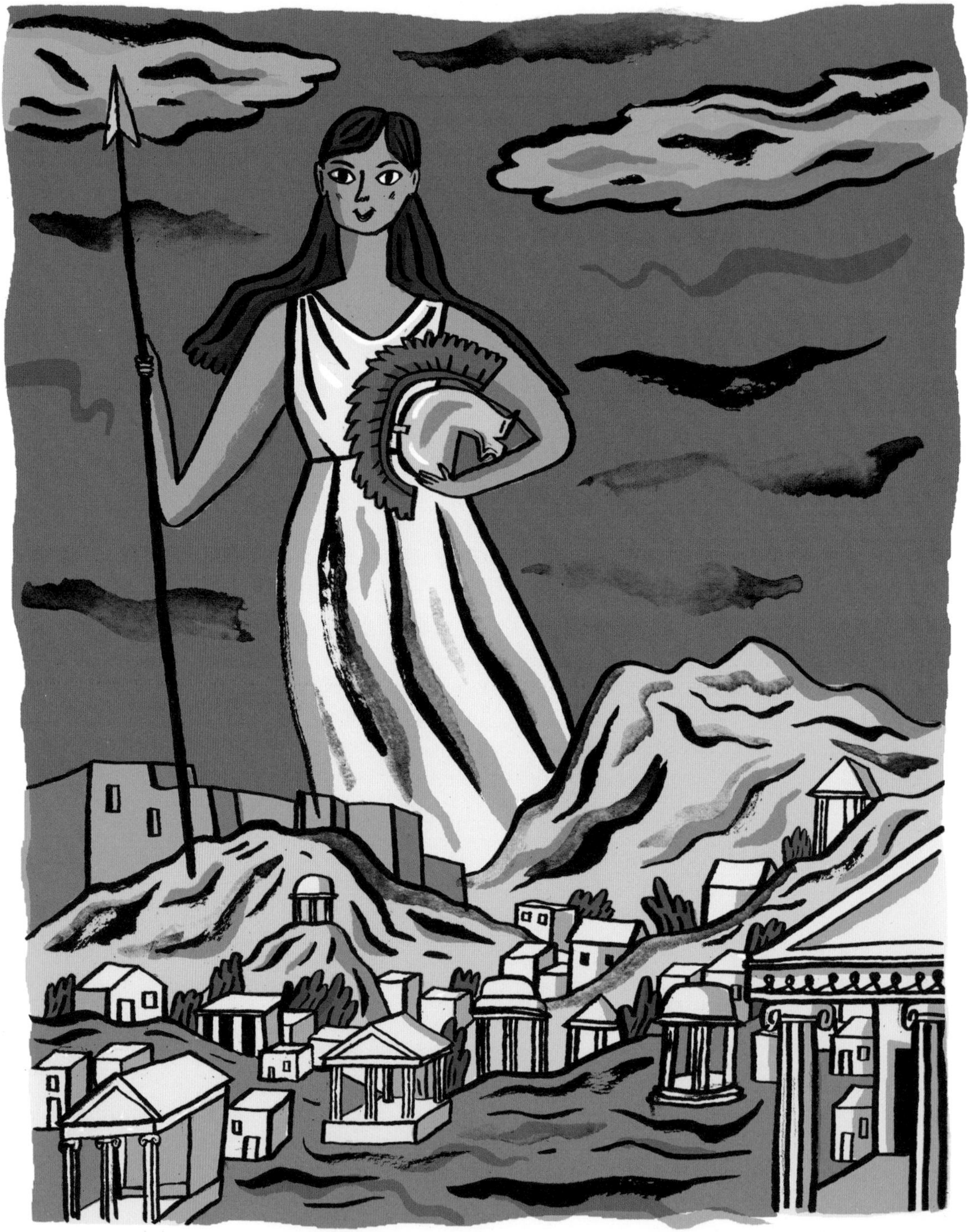

PART II

Erichthonius

ONE DAY, WHILE ATHENA WAS OUT HUNTING IN ATTICA, SHE CAME ACROSS A SMALL CHILD IN THE UNDERGROWTH. HIS SKIN GLOWED, AND SHE KNEW INSTANTLY THAT THIS WAS NO ORDINARY CHILD. HE WAS A DEMIGOD. BUT WHERE HAD THE CHILD COME FROM? BEFORE SHE HAD TIME TO THINK, ATHENA SAW HER BROTHER HEPHAESTUS COMING THROUGH THE WOODS. ATHENA DUCKED OUT OF SIGHT. HEPHAESTUS BEGAN SEARCHING IN THE UNDERGROWTH.

BEFORE HEPHAESTUS COULD COME ANY CLOSER, ATHENA TOOK THE CHILD AND RAN FURTHER INTO THE WOODS. THERE, SHE RAISED THE CHILD AS HER OWN. MANY YEARS PASSED, AND ATHENA SPENT MORE AND MORE TIME AWAY FROM MOUNT OLYMPUS.

THE OTHER GODS AND GODDESSES WONDERED WHERE SHE HAD GONE. ATHENA'S BROTHER HEPHAESTUS STILL COULDN'T FIND THE LITTLE BOY HE'D LOST IN THE WOODS, AND HE WONDERED ABOUT THIS TO HIMSELF. BUT THE DINNER TABLE ON MOUNT OLYMPUS WAS MUCH MORE PEACEFUL WITHOUT ATHENA QUARRELING WITH POSEIDON, SO THE FAMILY DIDN'T LOOK FOR HER. HERA, HER STEPMOTHER, KNEW THAT IF SHE WAS IN REAL TROUBLE, SHE'D COME TO HER FOR HELP.

ATHENA LIVED IN THE WOODS WITH HER BEAUTIFUL BOY, ERICHTHONIUS. TO PASS THE TIME, SHE INVENTED WEAVING: MAKING HUGE PICTURES FROM CLOTH (WHICH SHE CALLED TAPESTRIES) ON A SPECIAL MACHINE CALLED A LOOM. ATHENA WAS CRAFTY, AS WELL AS CLEVER, AND SOON SHE HAD WOVEN ENTIRE TAPESTRIES THAT TOLD THE STORY OF HER LIFE. ATHENA LOVED HER ADOPTED SON, BUT SHE MISSED THE FREEDOM OF THE SKIES AND THE SWEET AIR OF MOUNT OLYMPUS.

ONE DAY, A COUPLE IN ATHENS WENT INTO THE TEMPLE OF ATHENA AND PRAYED FOR A CHILD. THEY HAD TRIED FOR MANY YEARS, BUT NO CHILD HAD COME. ATHENA LISTENED TO THEIR DESPERATE PLEAS, AND AN IDEA CAME TO HER.

ERICHTHONIUS WOULD BE A GIFT TO THE CHILDLESS COUPLE, AND A GIFT TO THE CITY OF ATHENS. ON THE DAY THAT SHE DECIDED TO PART WITH HER LITTLE ONE, ATHENA WEPT SO MUCH THAT THE EARTH AROUND HER SHUDDERED. BUT SHE HAD DECIDED. LITTLE ERICHTHONIUS FOUND A NEW LIFE IN ATHENS, AND ATHENA RETURNED TO THE MOUNTAIN.

YEARS LATER, WHEN HE WAS KING OF ATHENS, AND RULED OVER THE CITY WITH KINDNESS AND HONOR, ATHENA KNEW SHE HAD DONE THE RIGHT THING.

PART III

Perseus and Medusa

ONCE ATHENA WAS BACK ON MOUNT OLYMPUS, SHE STARTED TO LOOK FOR A NEW ADVENTURE. IT JUST SO HAPPENED THAT A YOUNG DEMIGOD, PERSEUS—WHO WAS ALSO ATHENA'S HALF BROTHER—HAD FOUND HIMSELF IN A BIT OF A PICKLE. KING POLYDECTES HAD DEMANDED THAT PERSEUS BRING HIM THE HEAD OF MEDUSA, A POWERFUL GORGON. MANY ADVENTURERS HAD BEEN SENT ON THIS QUEST, BUT NONE HAD EVER RETURNED ALIVE. TERRIFYING TALES WERE TOLD ABOUT MEDUSA, AND IT WAS SAID THAT IF YOU LOOKED STRAIGHT INTO HER EYES, YOU TURNED TO STONE.

PERSEUS WAS BRAVE AND DETERMINED. BUT HE KNEW HE COULDN'T SUCCEED BY HIMSELF, SO HE CALLED ON ATHENA, KNOWING SHE WAS ONE OF THE BRAVEST GODDESSES. ATHENA KNEW SHE SHOULD HELP WITH THIS QUEST—BUT SHE DIDN'T KNOW HOW.

THIS SOUNDS DIFFICULT. IT'S BEST TO KNOW WHAT WE'RE UP AGAINST— LET'S GO VISIT THE NYMPHS. THEY MIGHT BE ABLE TO HELP!

34

THE PAIR TRAVELED TO AN ENCHANTED LAKE.
THERE, PERSEUS FOUND THE NYMPHS AND PERSUADED THEM TO HELP HIM.

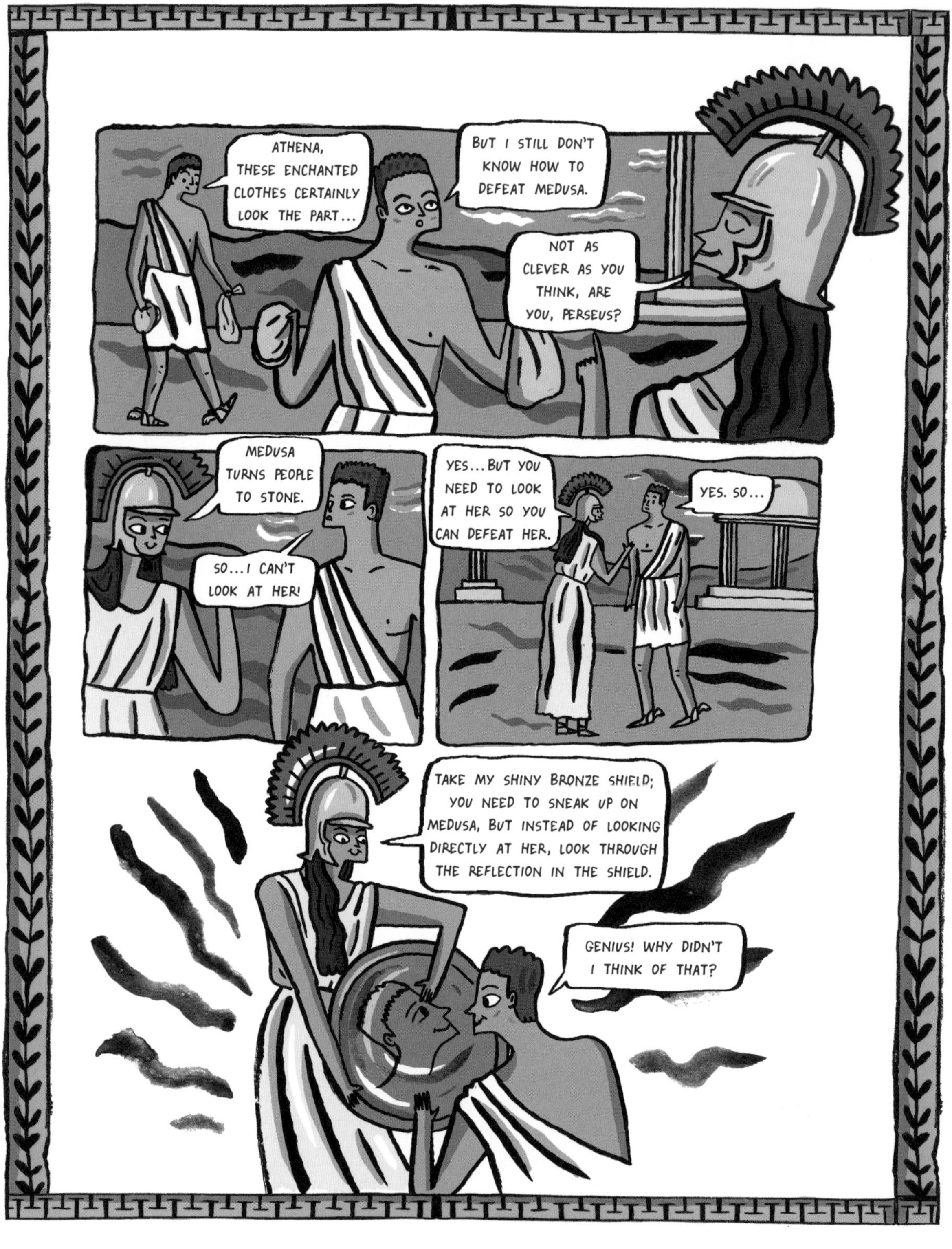
ATHENA, THESE ENCHANTED CLOTHES CERTAINLY LOOK THE PART...
BUT I STILL DON'T KNOW HOW TO DEFEAT MEDUSA.
NOT AS CLEVER AS YOU THINK, ARE YOU, PERSEUS?
MEDUSA TURNS PEOPLE TO STONE.
SO... I CAN'T LOOK AT HER!
YES... BUT YOU NEED TO LOOK AT HER SO YOU CAN DEFEAT HER.
YES. SO...
TAKE MY SHINY BRONZE SHIELD; YOU NEED TO SNEAK UP ON MEDUSA, BUT INSTEAD OF LOOKING DIRECTLY AT HER, LOOK THROUGH THE REFLECTION IN THE SHIELD.
GENIUS! WHY DIDN'T I THINK OF THAT?

WHEN PERSEUS REACHED THE GORGON'S CAVE, MEDUSA WAS SLEEPING.
PERSEUS EDGED INTO THE CAVE, AND PEEKED AT THE REFLECTION IN THE BRONZE SHIELD. HE SAW A FEARSOME SIGHT:
MEDUSA'S HEAD WAS COVERED IN WRIGGLING SNAKES, WITH BEADY EYES AND SLITHERING TONGUES. HE WAS TERRIFIED.

BUT ATHENA'S HAND GUIDED HIM SO HE KNEW WHICH WAY TO SWING HIS SWORD, AND HE CUT OFF MEDUSA'S HEAD.
HE QUICKLY THREW IT INTO THE BAG, AND—STILL WITHOUT LOOKING INTO HER EYES—RAN FROM THE CAVE.

THE HEADLESS MEDUSA WAS FURIOUS AND CHASED AFTER HIM. BUT PERSEUS WAS WEARING THE HAT
THAT MADE HIM INVISIBLE, AND HE HAD WINGS ON HIS SANDALS. HE WAS IMPOSSIBLE TO CATCH.

PERSEUS ARRIVED HOME TO THE CITY OF SERIPHOS, READY TO CELEBRATE HIS VICTORY.
BUT KING POLYDECTES HAD BECOME CRUEL AND DRIVEN PERSEUS'S FAMILY INTO HIDING. PERSEUS WAS LIVID;
HE MARCHED UP TO THE PALACE TO SEE THE KING. IN A VIOLENT TEMPER, THE KING RAN AT PERSEUS.
BUT PERSEUS PULLED OUT MEDUSA'S HEAD. POLYDECTES LOOKED STRAIGHT INTO HER EYES, AND HE TURNED TO STONE.

ATHENA, I
THINK YOU SHOULD TAKE
MEDUSA'S HEAD. I DON'T
TRUST ANYONE WITH IT,
NOT EVEN MYSELF.

THERE WAS PEACE IN THE CITY AT LAST. BUT PERSEUS NOW REALIZED HE HAD A TERRIBLE WEAPON AND WANTED ATHENA TO KEEP IT.

BESIDES, YOU WON
IT REALLY, NOT ME!

THIS LOOKS FEARSOME
ON MY SHIELD.

ATHENA RETURNED TO MOUNT OLYMPUS, TO SHOW OFF HER NEW SHIELD WITH THE HEAD
OF MEDUSA IN THE MIDDLE OF IT. PERSEUS RETURNED TO HIS OLD LIFE. IN MANY YEARS' TIME,
WITH THE WISDOM HE HAD LEARNED FROM ATHENA, AND AFTER MANY MORE ADVENTURES, HE BECAME A WISE KING.

PART IV

Arachne

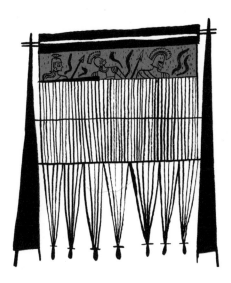

AFTER HELPING PERSEUS, ATHENA BECAME FAMOUS AMONG THE MORTALS. EVERY YOUNG WARRIOR WANTED ATHENA TO HELP WITH THEIR ADVENTURES. ALTHOUGH ATHENA HAD EARNED HER FAME, IT WAS STARTING TO GO TO HER HEAD AND SHE WAS GETTING A LITTLE BIT VAIN. HERA, THE WISEST OF ALL THE GODDESSES, WAS ABOUT TO GIVE HER SOME WORDS OF ADVICE, WHEN A YOUNG MORTAL CAUGHT ATHENA'S ATTENTION.

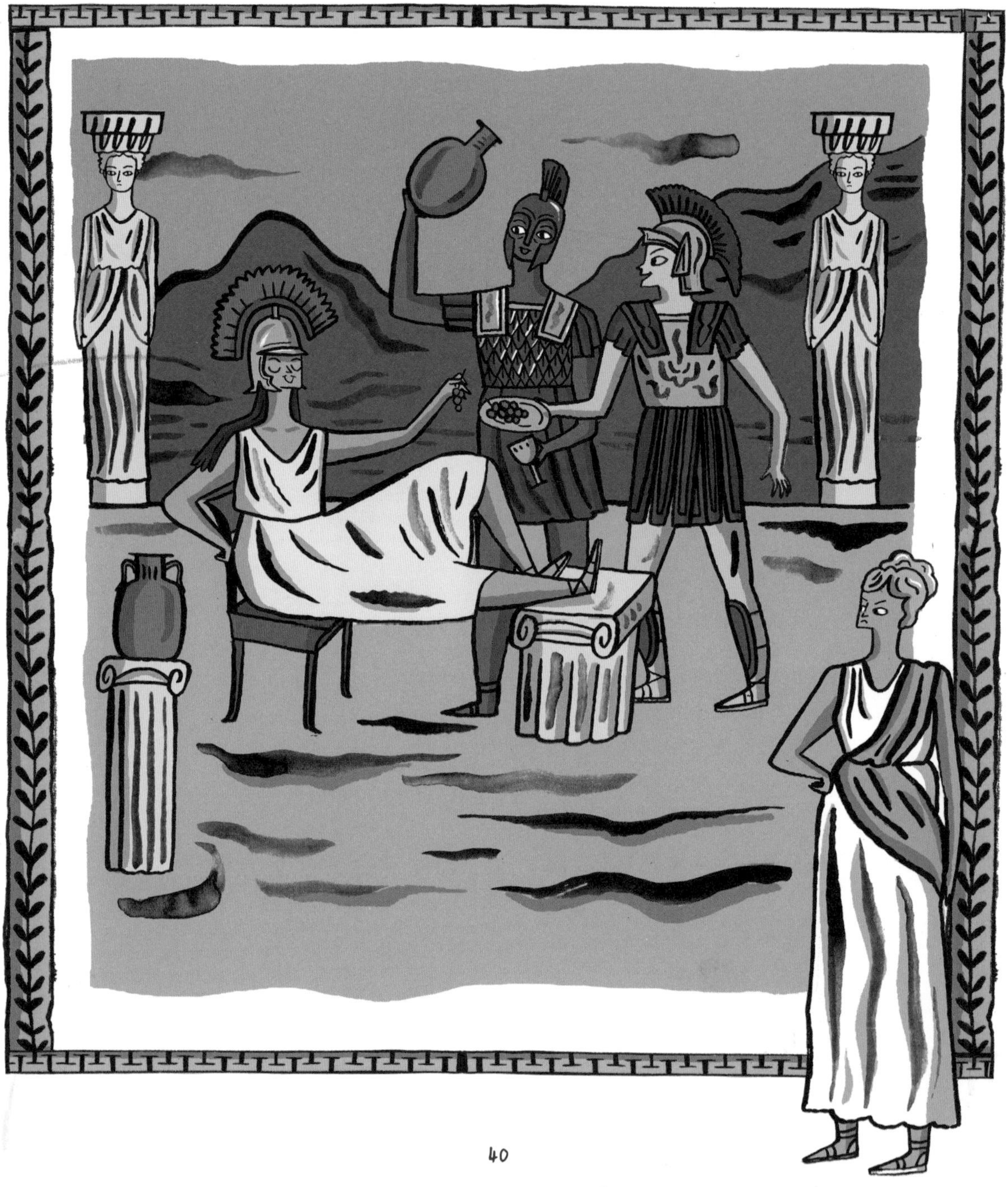

IN LYDIA THERE LIVED A YOUNG WOMAN NAMED ARACHNE, WHO WAS A SPECTACULAR WEAVER.
PEOPLE CAME FROM ALL OVER TO SEE HER WORK. ATHENA HEARD ABOUT ARACHNE'S WORK, AND SHE WAS
PLEASED THAT THE SKILLS SHE HAD INVENTED WERE BEING USED SO WELL. BUT AS ARACHNE SPUN MORE AND MORE,
SHE BECAME MORE AND MORE SURE THAT SHE WAS THE BEST WEAVER IN THE WORLD. AND SHE WANTED TO PROVE IT.

SHE WANTED TO CHALLENGE THE GREATEST WEAVER ON EARTH TO A SPIN-OFF. THERE WAS ONLY ONE PROBLEM: THERE WAS NO
GREATER WEAVER ON EARTH, ONLY ON MOUNT OLYMPUS. WHEN ATHENA HEARD THAT ARACHNE HAD CHALLENGED HER—THE GODDESS OF
CRAFT AND THE INVENTOR OF WEAVING—TO A SPIN-OFF, SHE LAUGHED. NO ONE COULD DEFEAT HER!

BUT SHE ALSO FELT SORRY FOR ARACHNE. ATHENA WAS CERTAIN SHE WOULD WIN, AND SHE DIDN'T WANT ARACHNE TO BE HUMILIATED, SO SHE DISGUISED HERSELF AS AN OLD WOMAN AND WENT TO VISIT YOUNG ARACHNE.

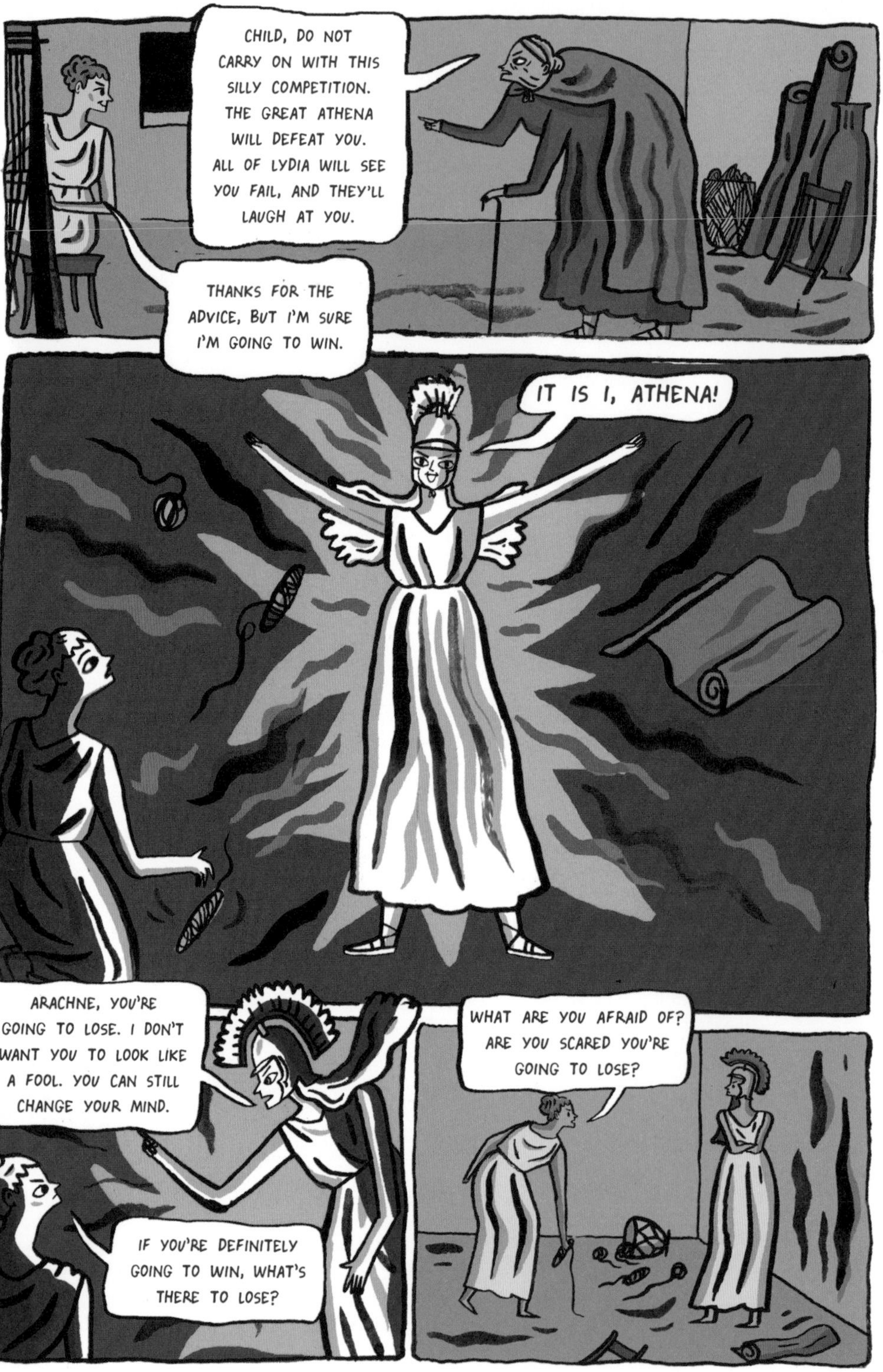

CHILD, DO NOT CARRY ON WITH THIS SILLY COMPETITION. THE GREAT ATHENA WILL DEFEAT YOU. ALL OF LYDIA WILL SEE YOU FAIL, AND THEY'LL LAUGH AT YOU.
THANKS FOR THE ADVICE, BUT I'M SURE I'M GOING TO WIN.
IT IS I, ATHENA!
ARACHNE, YOU'RE GOING TO LOSE. I DON'T WANT YOU TO LOOK LIKE A FOOL. YOU CAN STILL CHANGE YOUR MIND.
IF YOU'RE DEFINITELY GOING TO WIN, WHAT'S THERE TO LOSE?
WHAT ARE YOU AFRAID OF? ARE YOU SCARED YOU'RE GOING TO LOSE?

MAYBE ARACHNE WAS RIGHT: MAYBE ATHENA WAS A LITTLE BIT SCARED. BUT EITHER WAY,
THE COMPETITION WAS HAPPENING. THE OTHER GODS AND GODDESSES HEARD ABOUT THE COMPETITION,
AND THEY ALL CAME TO LYDIA TO WATCH IT. POSEIDON WAS IN THE FRONT ROW, CHEERING FOR ARACHNE. HE REALLY
WANTED TO WATCH ATHENA LOSE. THE COMPETITION BEGAN: ATHENA AND ARACHNE SHOOK HANDS. ATHENA, AS DEFENDER
OF THE TITLE, WOULD GO FIRST. SHE GATHERED UP HER WOOL AND BEGAN TO WEAVE. SHE SPUN LINE AFTER LINE
OF PERFECT THREAD, AND STARTED TO TWIRL THEM INTO A GREAT TAPESTRY, ON HER SPECIAL, SHINING LOOM.

SHE COULD SEE THE OTHER GODS CAREFULLY WATCHING HER, AND SHE WAS FURIOUS TO SEE POSEIDON CHEERING FOR HER
TO LOSE. SO SHE SPUN A PICTURE OF POSEIDON LOSING THE COMPETITION TO SPONSOR ATHENS, WHICH WAS ATHENA'S GREATEST
VICTORY SO FAR. SHE WAS SURE THIS WOULD IRRITATE POSEIDON. SMALLER SCENES WERE WOVEN INTO THE EDGES OF THE TAPESTRY.
ATHENA PICTURED MORTALS TRYING TO WIN AGAINST GODS, AND THE PUNISHMENT THEY FACED FOR BEING SO ARROGANT.
SHE WAS TRYING TO SCARE ARACHNE. HOW DARE SHE TRY TO COMPETE WITH A GODDESS!

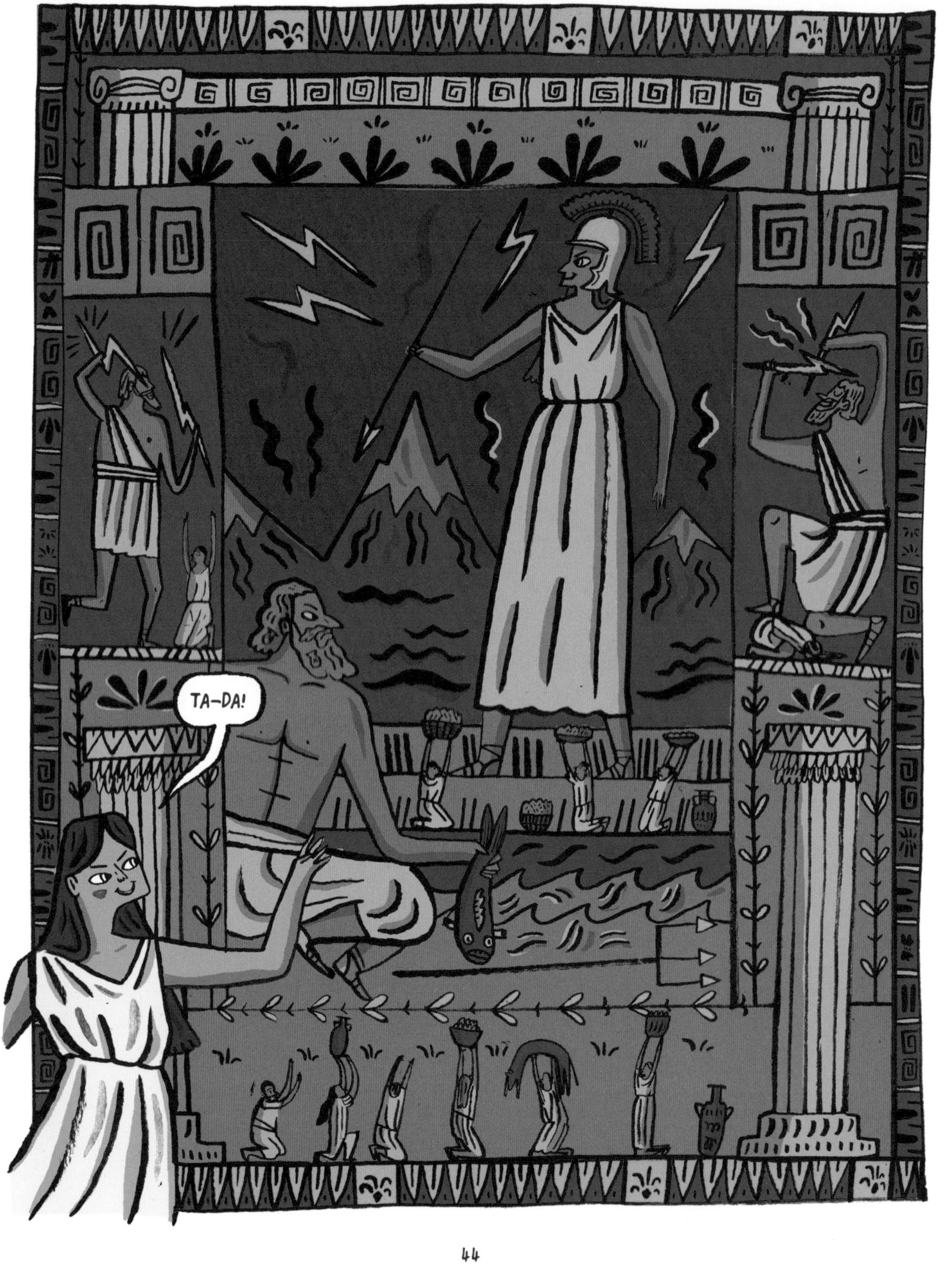
TA-DA!

WHEN ATHENA HAD FINISHED, ARACHNE STEPPED UP TO HER OWN LOOM, AND BEGAN TO SPIN.
EVEN ATHENA WAS AMAZED. SHE HAD NEVER SEEN ANYONE SPIN LIKE THIS BEFORE. ARACHNE BEGAN TO SPIN
HER THREADS INTO A PICTURE, AND ATHENA BECAME ANGRY. ARACHNE KNEW WHAT THE CROWD WANTED,
SO SHE STARTED TO WEAVE STORIES OF THE LOVE AFFAIRS BETWEEN THE GODS AND ORDINARY PEOPLE.

THE GODS WERE THRILLED TO SEE THEMSELVES, AND EVERY YOUNG MORTAL DREAMED OF BEING CHOSEN BY THE GODS.
THE CROWD WAS CAPTIVATED. EVERY SINGLE STITCH OF THE TAPESTRY WAS PERFECT. ARACHNE FINISHED AND STOOD UP
FROM HER LOOM. THE PEOPLE, THE GODS, AND THE GODDESSES ALL BROKE INTO DEAFENING APPLAUSE. ARACHNE HAD WON!

ATHENA WAS FURIOUS. IN A TERRIFYING RAGE,
SHE RIPPED ARACHNE'S TAPESTRY INTO TINY PIECES—BEFORE ANYONE COULD STOP HER.

AND SHE TURNED THE YOUNG GIRL INTO A SPIDER!

ATHENA STORMED BACK TO MOUNT OLYMPUS. WHEN SHE CALMED DOWN,
SHE BITTERLY REGRETTED WHAT SHE HAD DONE. BUT IT WAS ALREADY TOO LATE. FROM THAT DAY ON,
ATHENA WAS TERRIFIED OF SPIDERS, BECAUSE THEY REMINDED HER OF THE WORST THING SHE HAD EVER DONE.

PART V

Paris, Helen, and Troy

ATHENA MAY HAVE LEARNED HER LESSON, BUT HERA WAS FURIOUS WITH HER—THIS TIME
ATHENA'S VANITY REALLY HAD GONE TOO FAR. "ATHENA! YOU WERE TAUGHT TO HELP YOUNG MORTALS.
DO YOU EVER TRULY HELP MORTALS? OR DID YOU ONLY HELP PERSEUS SO THAT YOU WOULD BECOME EVEN
MORE FAMOUS? AND YOU'VE BEEN CRUEL TOWARD ARACHNE!" SHOUTED HERA.
"I'M SORRY. I KNOW IT WAS WRONG, BUT SHE WAS BEING SO...SILLY!" CRIED ATHENA. "ALL THOSE RIDICULOUS STORIES ABOUT LOVE!"
APHRODITE, THE GODDESS OF LOVE AND FERTILITY, HAD OVERHEARD HER SISTER AND NOW SHE WAS FURIOUS TOO!

"ATHENA!" INTERRUPTED APHRODITE, "EVERYBODY LIKED ARACHNE'S TAPESTRY MORE
THAN YOURS. THIS HAS NOTHING TO DO WITH LOVE—YOU JUST CAN'T STAND LOSING!"
"YOU'RE JEALOUS," SHOUTED ATHENA, "BECAUSE I'M BETTER AT SOMETHING THAN YOU!" HERA TRIED TO STOP THE FIGHT. BUT
IT WAS NO USE. THE ARGUMENT WAS GROWING LOUDER AND LOUDER. EVENTUALLY, THEY WOKE ZEUS, AND HE WASN'T HAPPY.
HE DEMANDED TO KNOW THE REASON FOR THE ARGUMENT, SO THAT HE COULD HAVE PEACE ON HIS MOUNTAIN ONCE MORE.

WHEN HE HEARD THAT ATHENA HAD TURNED A YOUNG WOMAN INTO A SPIDER, INSTEAD OF BEING ANGRY, HE WAS AMUSED!
NOW HERA WAS REALLY FURIOUS! NO WONDER ATHENA HAD LOST HER TEMPER. HER FATHER DIDN'T SCOLD HER—
EVEN WHEN SHE'D TURNED A MORTAL INTO A SPIDER. THE GIRLS CONTINUED TO BICKER, AND HERA STARTED SHOUTING
AT ZEUS. THE RUMBLES OF THEIR ARGUMENTS ECHOED THROUGH THE SKIES, UNTIL ZEUS SHOUTED.

HERA BEGAN TO PROTEST, BUT ZEUS ROARED WITH LAUGHTER, "HERA, PERHAPS YOU SHOULD COMPETE TOO!"
AND SO IT WAS DECIDED—ALL THREE GODDESSES WOULD COMPETE TO SEE WHO WAS THE BEST.
THE PRIZE WOULD BE THE GOLDEN APPLE OF ERIS. BUT HOW WOULD THEY DECIDE THE WINNER?

FOR SOME TIME, ZEUS HAD BEEN WATCHING A FOOLISH, COWARDLY YOUNG MAN NAMED PARIS. HE WAS THE PRINCE OF TROY: THE SON OF THE GREAT KING PRIAM OF THE KINGDOM OF TROY. ZEUS DECIDED THAT HE WOULD PUT PARIS TO THE TEST AND MAKE HIM DECIDE WHO WAS THE FAIREST OF THE THREE GODDESSES. ALL THEY HAD TO DO WAS CONVINCE HIM TO CHOOSE ONE OF THEM.

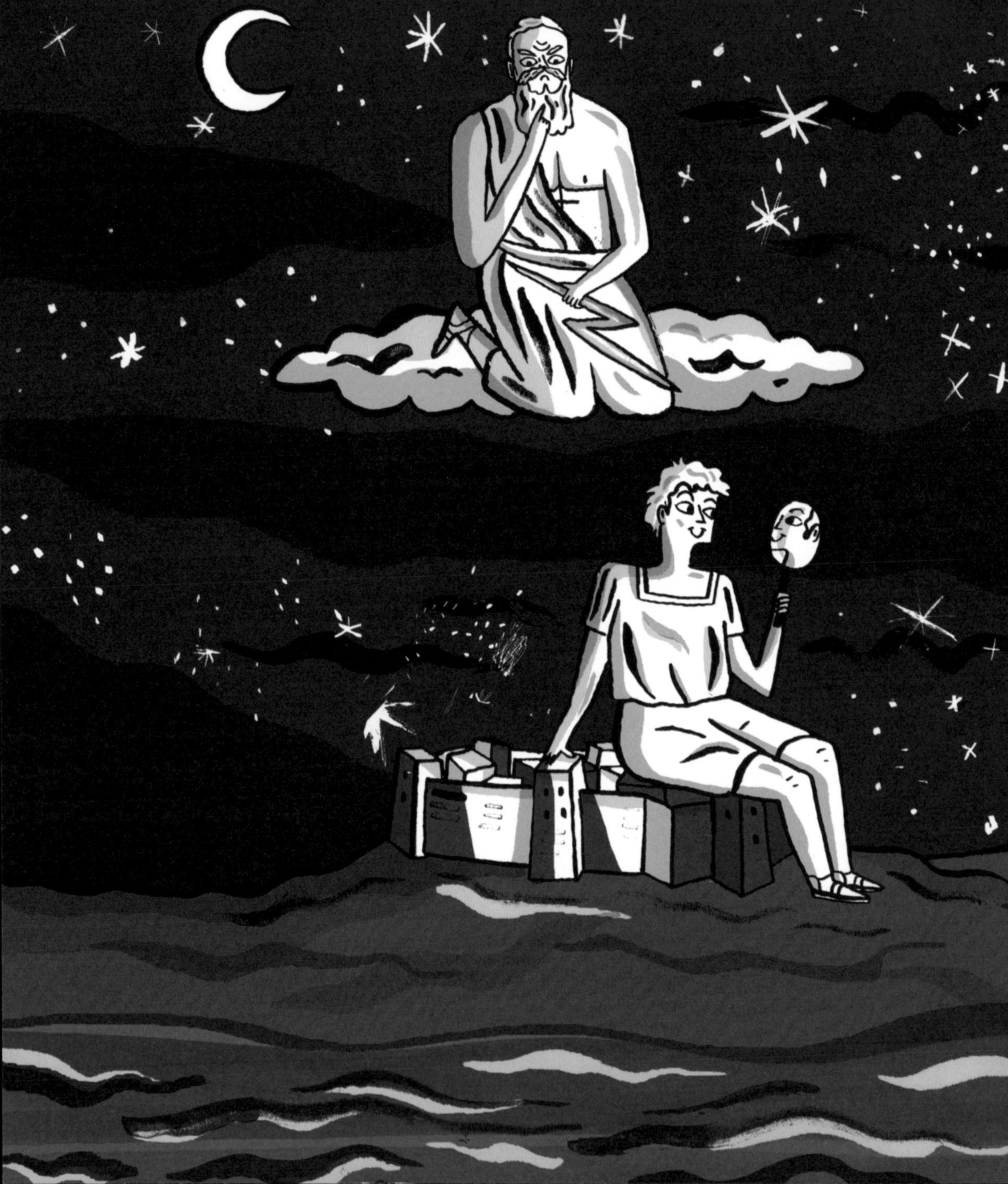

ATHENA WAS NOT IMPRESSED. "FAIREST?! BUT THAT IS NOT AS
IMPORTANT AS BEING CLEVER AND BRAVE! IT'S NOT A FAIR CONTEST!"
APHRODITE SIGHED AND WHISPERED, "THAT'S WHAT I'VE BEEN TRYING TO TELL YOU, ATHENA!
EVERYONE WANTS TO BE THE FAIREST, EXCEPT FOR YOU. WHICH IS WHY I'M GOING TO WIN."

HERMES TOOK THE THREE GODDESSES TO MOUNT IDA, WHERE PARIS WAS LOOKING AFTER HIS FLOCK OF SHEEP. HERMES APPEARED BEFORE PARIS AND CRIED, "PARIS! YOU HAVE BEEN CHOSEN BY THE MIGHTY ZEUS FOR THIS SPECIAL TASK. TELL US, WHO IS THE FAIREST GODDESS?" "OH, WOW. WHAT AN HONOR! I WISH I COULD CHOOSE ALL THREE," STAMMERED PARIS. "STOP BABBLING, PARIS," INTERRUPTED HERMES. "GODDESSES, IT IS TIME TO MAKE YOUR OFFERS TO THIS FINE YOUNG MAN." HERA STEPPED FORWARD. SHE WAS TALL AND INTIMIDATING, A TRUE QUEEN OF MOUNT OLYMPUS.

"PARIS. YOU ARE A FINE YOUNG MAN, AS HERMES SAYS," SHE BEGAN, "AND I CAN OFFER YOU POWER OVER THE ENTIRE WORLD. ALL YOU HAVE TO DO IS PICK ME OVER THE OTHER TWO." PARIS COULDN'T BELIEVE HIS LUCK.

ONE MINUTE, HE WAS MINDING HIS FLOCK, AND THE NEXT THE GREAT GODDESS HERA WAS OFFERING HIM WORLDWIDE POWER! IN HIS VANITY, HE HAD ALWAYS DREAMED OF THIS. HE WAS JUST ABOUT TO ACCEPT WHEN ATHENA STEPPED FORWARD. "PARIS. YOU ARE HANDSOME AND STRONG," SAID ATHENA, "BUT ARE YOU BRAVE AND CUNNING? HAVE YOU EVER BEEN TO WAR AND WON A BATTLE? HAVE YOU EVER HEARD OF PERSEUS? WELL, I'M THE GODDESS BEHIND ALL THE STORIES. PICK ME, AND YOU'LL HAVE ALL THE ADVENTURES YOU'VE EVER WANTED..."

PARIS WAS THRILLED. HE COULD ONLY DREAM OF BEING AS BRAVE—OR AS FAMOUS—AS THE GREAT HERO PERSEUS.

HE WAS JUST ABOUT TO ACCEPT ATHENA'S OFFER WHEN APHRODITE STEPPED FORWARD.
APHRODITE THOUGHT SHE SAW A GLINT IN PARIS'S EYE THAT SHE RECOGNIZED. PARIS WAS A HOPELESS ROMANTIC.
"PARIS, MY MOTHER CAN OFFER YOU POWER OVER THE ENTIRE WORLD. AND MY SISTER CAN OFFER YOU
VICTORIES AND FAME BEYOND YOUR WILDEST DREAMS. BUT WHAT WOULD IT MATTER, WITHOUT SOMEONE
TO LOVE BY YOUR SIDE?" APHRODITE CONTINUED, "PICK ME, AND THE MOST BEAUTIFUL WOMAN IN THE
WORLD SHALL BE YOURS TO LOVE AND TO MARRY."

PARIS'S EYES BEGAN TO WELL UP, AND HE LOOKED FULL OF LONGING AND HOPE. HERA WAS HORRIFIED. ATHENA WAS DISGUSTED.

PARIS HAD CHOSEN APHRODITE, AND SO AGAINST ALL ODDS, SHE HAD WON. BUT THERE WAS ONE SMALL PROBLEM. EVERYONE KNEW THAT THE MOST BEAUTIFUL WOMAN IN THE WORLD WAS HELEN OF SPARTA—AND SHE WAS ALREADY MARRIED TO KING MENELAUS.

PARIS WAS INCREDIBLY EXCITED TO MEET THE MOST BEAUTIFUL WOMAN IN THE WORLD.
APHRODITE KNEW THAT SHE COULDN'T TURN BACK ON HER PROMISE, SO SHE SENT PARIS AND HIS BROTHER HECTOR TO SPARTA. APHRODITE WORKED HER MAGIC, AND PARIS WAS INSTANTLY IN LOVE WITH HELEN—
AND HELEN WAS INSTANTLY IN LOVE WITH PARIS. APHRODITE BREATHED A SIGH OF RELIEF: WHAT COULD GO WRONG?

FATHER!

HM?

YOU CHOSE A STUPID, LOVESICK FOOL FOR OUR JUDGE! IT WASN'T A FAIR COMPETITION!

HE WAS ALWAYS GOING TO CHOSE APHRODITE!

IT'S ABOUT TIME YOU LEARNED A LESSON OR TWO.

MORTALS ARE FOOLS. AND YOU'VE BEEN MEDDLING IN THEIR ADVENTURES FOR FAR TOO LONG.

I HAVEN'T BEEN MEDDLING.

I'VE BEEN TRYING TO DO THE RIGHT THING.

AND YOU DID THE RIGHT THING WITH ARACHNE, EH?

OK! I MADE A MISTAKE, BUT...

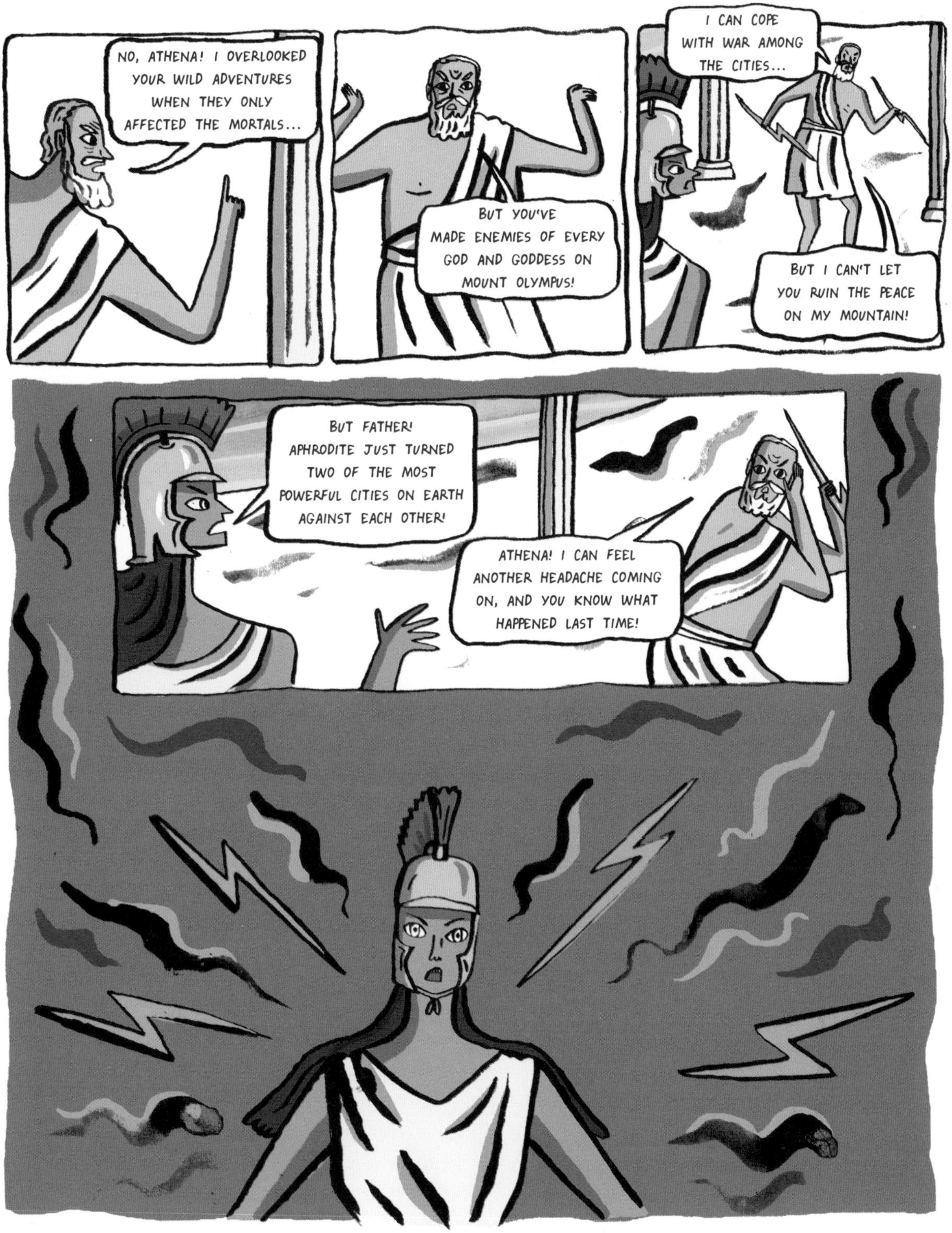
NO, ATHENA! I OVERLOOKED YOUR WILD ADVENTURES WHEN THEY ONLY AFFECTED THE MORTALS...
BUT YOU'VE MADE ENEMIES OF EVERY GOD AND GODDESS ON MOUNT OLYMPUS!
I CAN COPE WITH WAR AMONG THE CITIES...
BUT I CAN'T LET YOU RUIN THE PEACE ON MY MOUNTAIN!
BUT FATHER! APHRODITE JUST TURNED TWO OF THE MOST POWERFUL CITIES ON EARTH AGAINST EACH OTHER!
ATHENA! I CAN FEEL ANOTHER HEADACHE COMING ON, AND YOU KNOW WHAT HAPPENED LAST TIME!

BUT ATHENA WAS RIGHT TO BE WORRIED. HELEN HAD RUN AWAY WITH PARIS, IN THE MIDDLE OF THE NIGHT, AND SAILED TO TROY. HELEN'S HUSBAND, KING MENELAUS, WAS FURIOUS. HIS BROTHER AGAMEMNON, THE KING OF MYCENAE, WAS BUILDING AN EPIC ARMY FROM ALL OF THE GREEK CITIES AND ISLANDS. TOGETHER THEY WERE GOING TO WAGE WAR ON TROY. THEY WERE DETERMINED TO GET HELEN BACK AND DEFEAT THE TROJANS ONCE AND FOR ALL.

ATHENA WENT TO TROY, AND BY THE TIME SHE ARRIVED, THE GREEKS HAD SET UP CAMP ON THE BEACH. FOR MILES AND MILES, THERE WERE TENTS, WARRIORS, HORSES, AND ARMOR. AS A RESULT, THE TROJANS HAD RETREATED INSIDE THE WALLS OF TROY.

PART VI

The Trojan Horse

EVERY DAY FOR THE NEXT TEN YEARS, THE TROJAN AND THE GREEK ARMIES FOUGHT ON THE BEACH. THE GODS AND GODDESSES HADN'T LEARNED THEIR LESSON, AND THEY ALL BEGAN TO GET INVOLVED IN THE WAR. APHRODITE WAS ON THE SIDE OF THE TROJANS. SHE HAD TO HELP THE YOUNG COUPLE AND PROVE THAT LOVE REALLY WAS THE MOST IMPORTANT THING OF ALL. ATHENA WAS ON THE SIDE OF THE GREEKS, OF COURSE, AND HERA WAS HELPING HER TRY TO FIX THIS MESS.

THE WAR RAGED ON, AND ATHENA MARCHED INTO BATTLE WITH THE GREEK ARMIES, FIGHTING ALONGSIDE THEM EVEN ON THE DARKEST DAYS OF BATTLE. THE GREEKS WERE LED BY THE UNDEFEATABLE ACHILLES, A GREAT WARRIOR. PARIS, PRINCE OF TROY, WAS HANDSOME, BUT HE WAS NOT BRAVE IN BATTLE. SO HIS BROTHER HECTOR COMMANDED THE TROJAN ARMIES IN HIS PLACE.

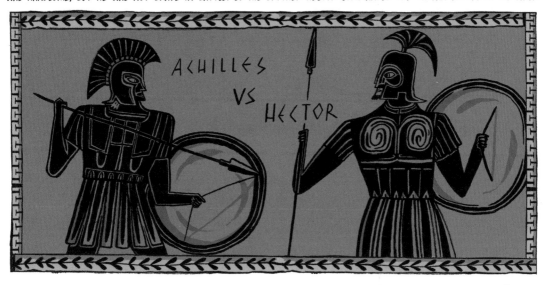

ONE DAY, THE UNDEFEATABLE ACHILLES WAS KILLED IN BATTLE BY PRINCE HECTOR. EVERYONE WAS SHOCKED! THIS HAD TO BE A TRICK. AND IT WAS. PATROCLUS, THE CLOSEST FRIEND OF ACHILLES, HAD DRESSED IN HIS ARMOR. HECTOR HAD ACCIDENTALLY KILLED PATROCLUS! ACHILLES DEMANDED REVENGE, AND IN AN EPIC ONE-ON-ONE BATTLE, HE KILLED HECTOR.

PARIS WAS DEVASTATED. HIS BROTHER WAS DEAD, AND HE THOUGHT IT WAS HIS FAULT. HE WANTED REVENGE. PARIS HAD HEARD A STORY ABOUT ACHILLES: HIS MOTHER HAD BATHED HIM IN THE POWERFUL RIVER STYX AS A BABY, AND THAT'S WHAT MADE HIM UNDEFEATABLE. BUT SINCE SHE HAD DANGLED HIM BY HIS ANKLE, THERE WAS A SINGLE SPOT WHERE SHE HAD HELD HIM THAT WASN'T INVINCIBLE.

FROM THE HIGH WALLS OF TROY, PARIS'S ARROW SHOT STRAIGHT THROUGH ACHILLES'S HEEL, THE ONLY WEAK SPOT HE HAD. ACHILLES FELL TO THE GROUND AND WAS KILLED.

ATHENA WAS FURIOUS THAT ACHILLES,
ONE OF HER FAVORED WARRIORS AND THE LEADER OF THE GREEKS, HAD DIED.
WITH ACHILLES GONE, THE GREEKS NOW NEEDED A NEW WARRIOR. ATHENA HAD
BEEN WATCHING A YOUNG GREEK MAN FROM ITHAKA, NAMED ODYSSEUS.
HE WASN'T THE LARGEST WARRIOR, OR THE STRONGEST, OR THE MOST FEARSOME,
BUT HE WAS SMART, AND ATHENA SOON PERSUADED THE GREEKS TO CHOOSE
ODYSSEUS AS THEIR NEW CHAMPION.

AFTER TEN LONG YEARS OF WAR, THE ARMIES WERE AT A STALEMATE. THE GREEKS COULDN'T GET PAST THE TROJAN WALLS, AND THE TROJANS DIDN'T HAVE ENOUGH MEN TO DEFEAT THE GREEK ARMY.

ATHENA WAS GETTING IMPATIENT. SHE HAD A BRILLIANT IDEA AND DECIDED IT WAS TIME TO GIVE IT TO ODYSSEUS. AND SO, AS IF BY MAGIC, ODYSSEUS CAME UP WITH A CUNNING PLAN: INSTEAD OF LURING THE TROJANS OUT, THEY WOULD FORCE THE TROJANS TO LET THE GREEKS IN.

WHEN THE TROJANS WOKE THE NEXT MORNING,
THE GREEK SHIPS WERE GONE. INSTEAD OF A CAMP ON THE BEACH,
THERE WAS AN ENORMOUS WOODEN HORSE. THE TROJANS DECIDED
IT WAS A GIFT FROM THE GODS, AND THIS MEANT THE WAR WAS
OVER AT LAST! THEY BROUGHT THE HORSE INTO THE CITY
AND CELEBRATED ALL DAY AND NIGHT.

BUT THE TROJANS DIDN'T
KNOW THAT THE GREEK SOLDIERS WERE
HIDING INSIDE THE HORSE! AND WHILE
THE TROJANS WERE SLEEPING, TIRED FROM
CELEBRATING ALL EVENING, THE GREEKS
CLIMBED OUT AND DESTROYED THE CITY.
AND SO THE GREEKS DEFEATED THE TROJANS.
APHRODITE WAS FURIOUS. HELEN HAD TO
LEAVE PARIS AND RETURN TO GREECE WITH
HER HUSBAND, MENELAUS. LOVE HAD NOT
CONQUERED AFTER ALL!

BUT THE STORY WASN'T QUITE FINISHED YET...

PART VII

Odysseus's Adventures

THE GREEKS CELEBRATED THEIR VICTORY, THEN PACKED UP THEIR CAMP AND LEFT TROY. ODYSSEUS AND HIS MEN SET OFF AFTER THE OTHER COMMANDERS. WITHIN HOURS OF SETTING SAIL, A GREAT STORM HAD BLOWN THE SAILORS OFF COURSE. ATHENA BLAMED POSEIDON, WHO ALWAYS TRIED TO CREATE TROUBLE FOR HER AND HER MORTALS.

ODYSSEUS HAD A WIFE AND SON IN ITHAKA, AND MORE THAN ANYTHING—MORE THAN ADVENTURES AND VICTORIES AND EVERLASTING FAME—HE WANTED TO SEE THEM AGAIN. BOTH ATHENA AND APHRODITE DECIDED THEY WOULD HELP: ATHENA WOULD HELP ODYSSEUS AND HIS MEN OVERCOME THE TERRIBLE CHALLENGES AHEAD, AND OUTSMART HER UNCLE POSEIDON, BECAUSE IT WAS A GREAT ADVENTURE AND AN EPIC STORY. APHRODITE AGREED TO HELP BECAUSE SHE WAS SO IMPRESSED WITH ODYSSEUS: ALL HE WANTED NOW WAS THE LOVE OF HIS FAMILY. AFTER YEARS OF ARGUMENTS—AND A LONG MORTAL WAR—THE SISTERS WERE BACK ON THE SAME SIDE AGAIN.

MEANWHILE IN ITHAKA, ODYSSEUS'S FAMILY WERE WORRIED. HIS SON AND WIFE, TELEMACHUS
AND PENELOPE, WERE HAVING A TERRIBLE TIME. EVERYONE THOUGHT ODYSSEUS WAS DEAD,
AND SUITORS BEGAN TO ARRIVE JUST WEEKS AFTER THE REST OF THE GREEKS RETURNED,
ALL HOPING TO MARRY PENELOPE. THEY SPENT YEARS IN THE PALACE WAITING FOR PENELOPE TO
GIVE UP ON ODYSSEUS. ATHENA WENT BACK TO ITHAKA MANY TIMES OVER THE NEXT TEN YEARS,
IN LOTS OF DIFFERENT DISGUISES. SHE DROVE AWAY SUITORS, HELPED PENELOPE TO SLEEP EASILY,
AND MENTORED TELEMACHUS, PROMISING HIM THAT HIS FATHER WOULD COME HOME.

ZEUS WAS STILL ANGRY AND WATCHED ATHENA CLOSELY TO MAKE SURE SHE DIDN'T
MEDDLE TOO MUCH MORE. SO SHE HAD TO LET ODYSSEUS FIND HIS OWN WAY HOME.
SHE WOULD WATCH CLOSELY AND INTERVENE ONLY IF SHE REALLY, REALLY NEEDED TO.

WHILE LOST AT SEA, ODYSSEUS AND HIS MEN CAME ACROSS AN ISLAND.
ODYSSEUS AND TWELVE MEN WENT AHEAD TO MAKE SURE IT WAS SAFE. THEY FOUND A CAVE FILLED WITH GOATS, SHEEP, AND FOOD.
THE MEN WERE SCARED, BUT ODYSSEUS WAS SURE THE OWNER WOULD SHARE WITH THEM.

UNFORTUNATELY, THE CAVE WAS HOME TO
A FEROCIOUS CYCLOPS, A GIANT WITH A SINGLE
EYE IN THE MIDDLE OF HIS FOREHEAD.

THE CYCLOPS ATE TWO OF THE MEN AS SOON
AS HE SAW THEM, THEN TWO MORE THE NEXT
MORNING, AND ANOTHER TWO THE NEXT NIGHT.

AT THIS RATE,
WE'LL ALL BE DEAD IN
A FEW DAYS!

SO ODYSSEUS CAME UP WITH ANOTHER CLEVER PLAN. HE WAS CARRYING SOME SWEET WINE,
AND HE OFFERED THIS TO THE CYCLOPS. AND THE CYCLOPS DRANK IT ALL.

WHAT'S YOUR NAME?

MY NAME IS NOBODY...

WHEN THE GIANT FELL ASLEEP, ODYSSEUS AND HIS
MEN DROVE A SHARP STAKE THROUGH HIS EYE.
THE CYCLOPS WAS BLINDED AND ROARED IN PAIN,
CALLING FOR THE OTHER CYCLOPES TO COME AND HELP.
BUT ODYSSEUS WAS SHOWING OFF, AND SHOUTED
HIS REAL NAME BACK TO THE CYCLOPS.

WHAT'S GOING ON?!

NOBODY IS TRYING TO KILL ME!

ODYSSEUS! THE MAN WHO BESTED YOU IS THE CUNNING ODYSSEUS!

THE MONSTER WAS FURIOUS AND DEMANDED REVENGE.
HE TURNED TO POSEIDON FOR HELP. POSEIDON WAS ONLY TOO HAPPY TO HELP, AND BREWED UP ANOTHER
STORM THAT TOSSED ODYSSEUS AND HIS MEN OFF COURSE.

SOON THEY FOUND ANOTHER ISLAND. THEY MOORED THE SHIP, AND ODYSSEUS'S MEN WENT AHEAD TO SEARCH THE LAND, WHILE ODYSSEUS STAYED ON THE BOAT. IN THE FOREST, THEY FOUND A BEAUTIFUL AND SECLUDED HOME. LIONS AND WOLVES GUARDED THE HOUSE, BUT THEY WERE NOT FEROCIOUS ANIMALS, AND INSTEAD THEY WAGGED THEIR TAILS AND ROLLED OVER TO BE STROKED. THERE WAS SOMETHING STRANGE GOING ON HERE!

THERE WAS MUSIC INSIDE THE HOUSE, AND SOMEONE WAS SINGING SWEETLY—THIS WAS THE HOME OF CIRCE, DAUGHTER OF THE SUN GOD HELIOS. SHE INSTANTLY TURNED ALL OF THE MEN INTO PIGS, EXCEPT FOR ONE MAN WHO ESCAPED BACK TO THE BOAT AND WARNED ODYSSEUS.

ODYSSEUS AND HIS MEN SET OUT TO SAVE THE MAN-ANIMALS. ATHENA WAS WATCHING FROM AFAR, AND WAS GROWING MORE AND MORE FRUSTRATED THAT SHE COULD NOT GET INVOLVED. SHE COULDN'T JUST WATCH ODYSSEUS BE TURNED INTO A PIG! SO SHE SENT HERMES TO VISIT HIM.

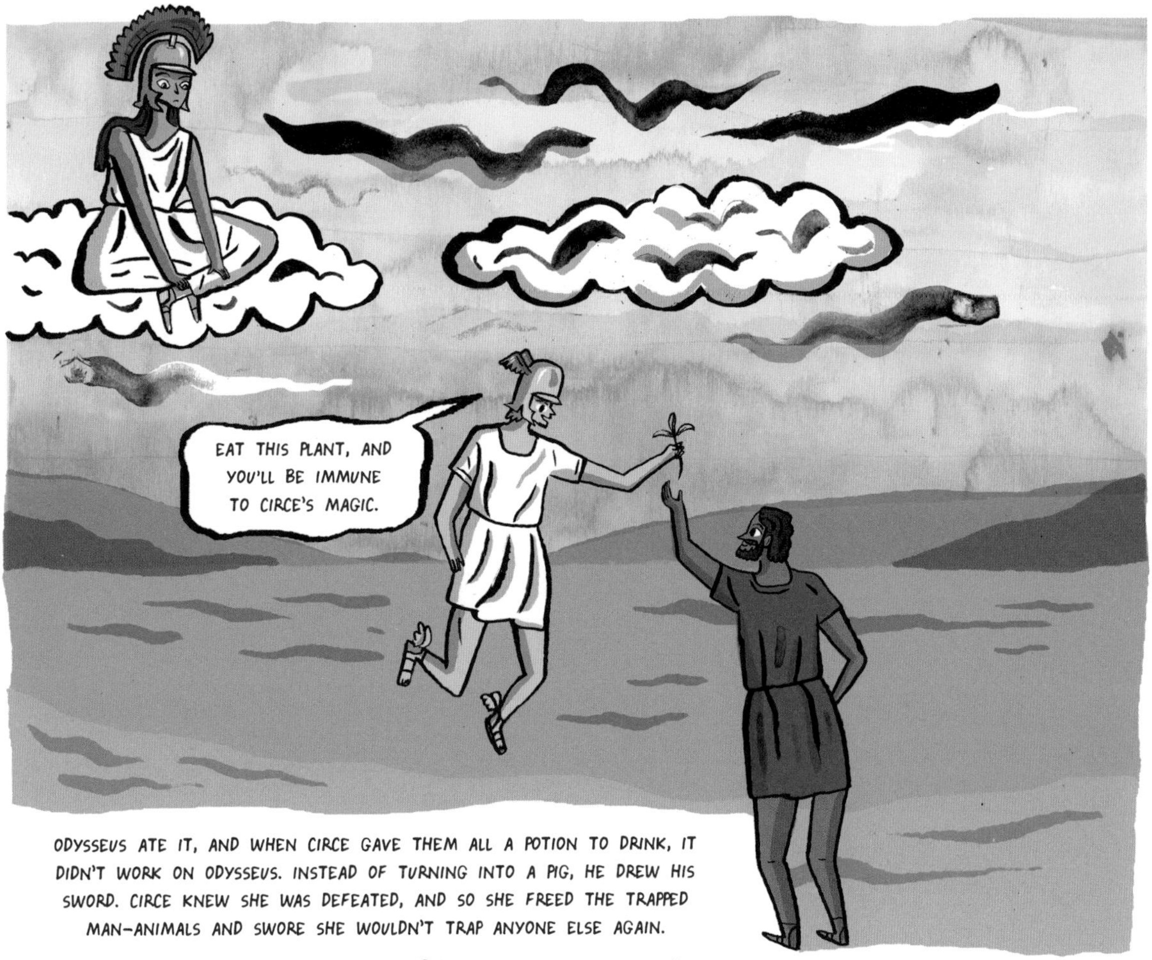
EAT THIS PLANT, AND YOU'LL BE IMMUNE TO CIRCE'S MAGIC.

ODYSSEUS ATE IT, AND WHEN CIRCE GAVE THEM ALL A POTION TO DRINK, IT DIDN'T WORK ON ODYSSEUS. INSTEAD OF TURNING INTO A PIG, HE DREW HIS SWORD. CIRCE KNEW SHE WAS DEFEATED, AND SO SHE FREED THE TRAPPED MAN-ANIMALS AND SWORE SHE WOULDN'T TRAP ANYONE ELSE AGAIN.

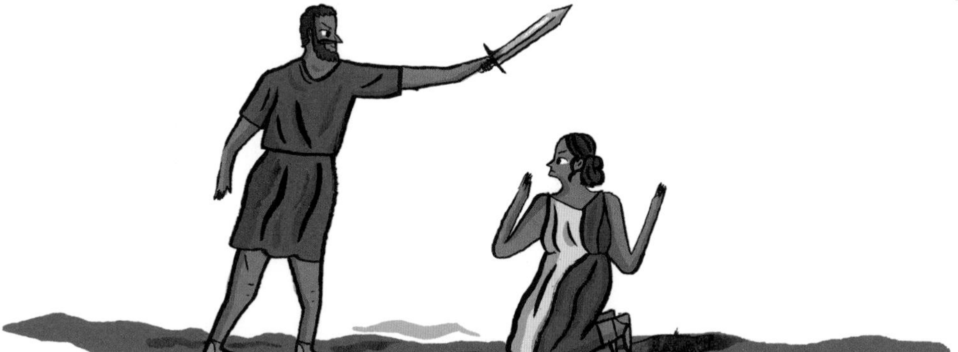

ODYSSEUS AND HIS MEN SETTLED ON THE ISLAND TO GATHER THEIR STRENGTH. THEY WERE HAVING A WONDERFUL TIME FEASTING AND DRINKING, AND BEFORE THEY KNEW IT, A YEAR HAD PASSED. THEY WERE WELL FED AND RESTED, BUT THIS ISLAND WASN'T THEIR HOME. "WE REALLY MUST GO," ODYSSEUS COMMANDED, "WE'VE WASTED ENOUGH TIME!"

THEY SET SAIL, AND BEFORE LONG, THEY HEARD SINGING AGAIN. IT WAS COMING FROM THE ROCKS OF AN ISLAND NEARBY. SIRENS, BEAUTIFUL BUT TERRIBLE CREATURES, WERE ENCHANTING THEM WITH THEIR SONG, LURING THEM ONTO THE ROCKS. ODYSSEUS TOLD HIS MEN TO PUT BEESWAX IN THEIR EARS, SO THEY COULDN'T HEAR THE SONG. THEN HE COMMANDED THEM TO TIE HIM TO THE MAST OF THE SHIP, SO THAT HE COULD HEAR THE SIRENS' SONG, WHICH WOULD PREDICT THE FUTURE. THEY SAILED ON TO SAFETY, AND ODYSSEUS WAS THE ONLY MAN EVER TO SURVIVE THE SIRENS' SONGS.

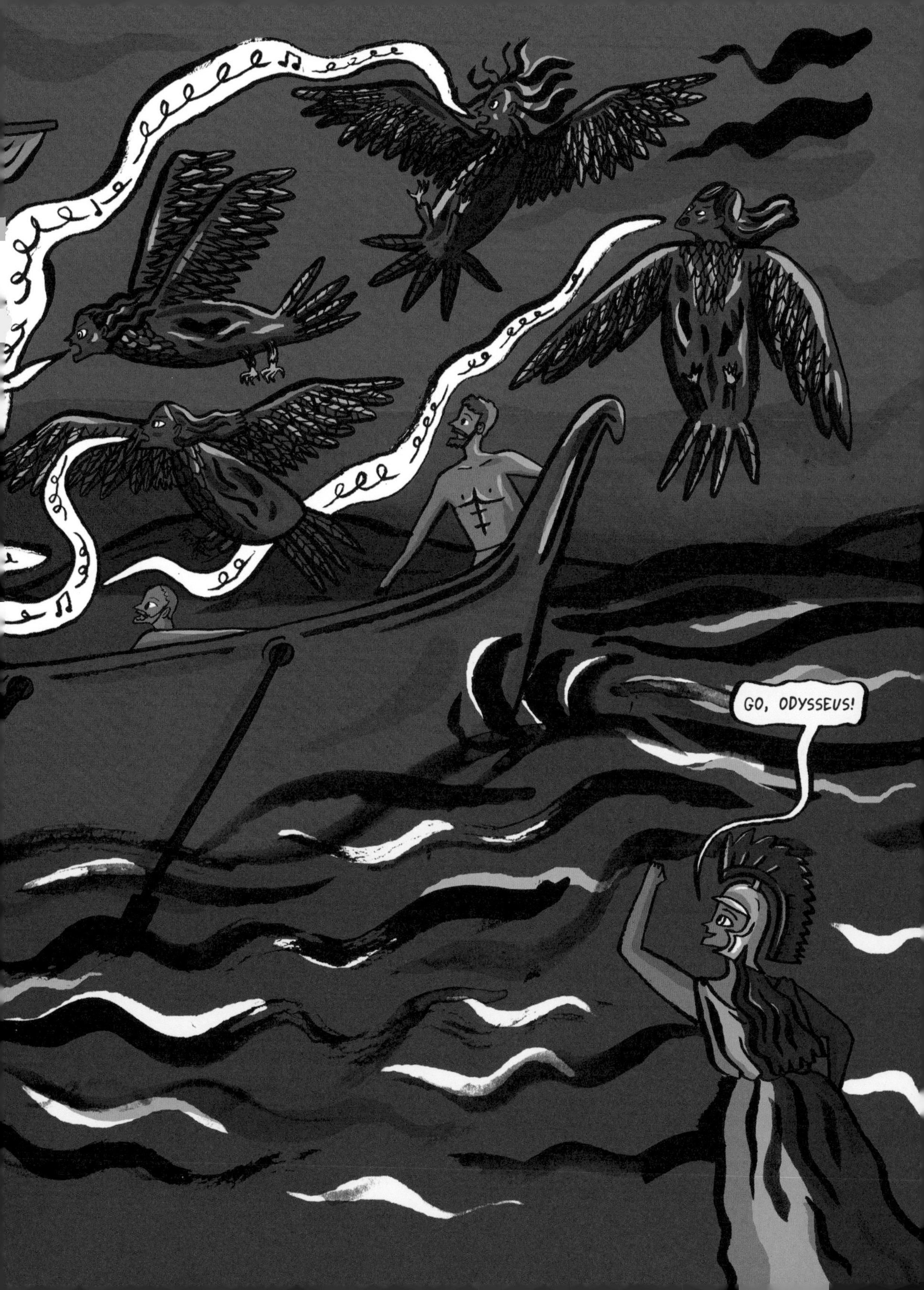
GO, ODYSSEUS!

THE NEXT ISLAND WAS FULL OF CATTLE.
THE MEN CRIED WITH JOY. THEY WERE STARVING! BUT ODYSSEUS STOPPED THEM,
"THESE CATTLE BELONG TO THE SUN GOD HELIOS, CIRCE'S FATHER. SHE SAID WE MUST NEVER, EVER EAT THEM.
BUT DON'T WORRY, I'LL GO FISHING FOR OUR DINNER."

AS SOON AS ODYSSEUS LEFT, THE MEN FELT FAR TOO HUNGRY TO WAIT,
SO THEY KILLED A COW AND ATE IT. WHEN HE RETURNED,
ODYSSEUS WAS FURIOUS. NOW THEY'D ALL HAVE TO TRY TO ESCAPE!
THEY RAN BACK TO THEIR SHIPS AND LEFT, HOPING THAT NOBODY HAD NOTICED.

BUT HELIOS HAD NOTICED, AND HE WAS ANGRY. HE WENT STRAIGHT TO ZEUS,
WHO KNEW HE HAD TO PUNISH THEM. HE SENT A GREAT STORM AFTER THEM,
AND THIS TIME ALL OF THE MEN DROWNED, EXCEPT FOR ODYSSEUS.

THERE, THE BEAUTIFUL CALYPSO FELL IN LOVE WITH HIM,
AND THERE HE STAYED FOR SEVEN LONG YEARS, UNDER HER SPELL. BUT THE LONGER HE STAYED,
THE MORE HE WANTED TO GO HOME.

FINALLY IT WAS TIME FOR ATHENA TO INTERVENE. WHILE POSEIDON WAS BUSY ON THE OTHER SIDE OF THE WORLD, ATHENA WENT TO ZEUS AND PLEADED WITH HIM TO LET HER HELP ODYSSEUS GET HOME. ZEUS AGREED AND PERSUADED CALYPSO TO RELEASE ODYSSEUS.

FOR SEVENTEEN DAYS, ODYSSEUS SAILED THE SEAS TOWARD HOME. BUT ON THE EIGHTEENTH DAY, POSEIDON RETURNED AND SENT A TERRIBLE STORM AFTER HIM. THIS TIME, ODYSSEUS ALMOST DROWNED.

AT LONG LAST, ATHENA GUIDED HIM ON BOARD A SHIP WITH SOME KIND SAILORS, HEADING FOR ITHAKA ONCE MORE.
ATHENA WAS THERE TO MEET HIM. ATHENA CRIED, "TWENTY YEARS I'VE BEEN WATCHING OVER YOU, ODYSSEUS!
BUT BEFORE WE GET REVENGE ON THE SUITORS, THERE'S SOMEONE WHO WANTS TO SEE YOU." ATHENA BROUGHT TELEMACHUS
TO SEE HIS FATHER. TELEMACHUS WAS JUST A BOY WHEN HIS FATHER SAILED FOR TROY, AND HE WAS NOW A YOUNG MAN.
THEY WERE SO HAPPY TO SEE EACH OTHER, THEY WEPT AND HUGGED AND LAUGHED.

NOW, IT WAS TIME FOR ODYSSEUS TO RETURN HOME. ATHENA DISGUISED ODYSSEUS AS AN OLD BEGGAR,
AND HE SET OFF FOR THE PALACE. THE SUITORS WERE FEASTING AND DRINKING AND ACTING LIKE THEY OWNED THE PALACE.
ATHENA SENT PENELOPE TO THE GREAT HALL TO MAKE AN ANNOUNCEMENT.

SUITORS! IT HAS BEEN TWENTY YEARS AND I AM CONVINCED THAT MY HUSBAND HAS DIED AT SEA. SO I SHALL MARRY ONE OF YOU.

THERE SHALL BE A COMPETITION TOMORROW.

THE NEXT DAY, THE CONTEST BEGAN. ALL THEY HAD TO DO WAS STRING ODYSSEUS'S GREAT BOW AND SHOOT A BULL'S-EYE, RIGHT IN THE MIDDLE OF THE TARGET. FIRST UP WAS THE MYSTERIOUS OLD MAN. HE DID IT PERFECTLY IN ONE SHOT! THE SUITORS WERE ALREADY SUSPICIOUS. THEN, ATHENA SUDDENLY TURNED ODYSSEUS BACK INTO HIMSELF, AND ODYSSEUS AND TELEMACHUS FOUGHT AND KILLED EVERY LAST SUITOR FOR TAKING ADVANTAGE OF THEIR HOME AND THEIR TROUBLES.

WHEN PENELOPE HEARD THAT HER HUSBAND HAD RETURNED, SHE DIDN'T BELIEVE IT. WHEN SHE FINALLY SAW HIM, SHE WEPT AND SHE HUGGED HIM. SHE WAS ANGRY THAT HE HAD TAKEN SO LONG TO COME HOME, OF COURSE. BUT SHE FORGAVE HIM. ODYSSEUS HAD FOUND HIS WAY HOME AND WON BACK THE LOVE OF PENELOPE AND TELEMACHUS.

ATHENA HAD LEARNED TO ADVISE AND HELP THE MORTALS BUT TO ONLY GET INVOLVED WHEN THEY CALLED ON HER. AND TO ONLY INTERVENE FOR THE BEST OF CAUSES. SHE AND APHRODITE HAD MADE UP AT LAST, BECAUSE THEY HAD SEEN WHAT TRUE ADVENTURING AND TRUE LOVE LOOKED LIKE. IT WASN'T FOR FAME OR FORTUNE, IT WAS FOR HOME. HERA WAS VERY PROUD OF THEM AND ALL THAT THEY HAD LEARNED. AND THE THREE OF THEM WERE VERY PLEASED THAT THEY HAD FINALLY TAUGHT UNCLE POSEIDON A LESSON!

GLOSSARY

ATHENS: The capital and the largest city in Greece. Athena is its patron goddess.

ATTICA: A peninsula in Greece that juts into the Aegean Sea. Athens is within Attica.

BLACKSMITH: A person who creates and repairs metal objects.

CYCLOPS: A one-eyed giant. They tend to live a simple life, sleeping in caves and herding sheep and goats.

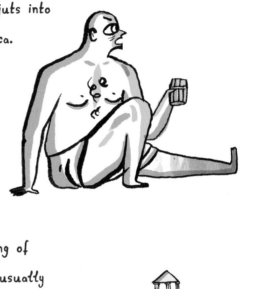

DEMIGOD: A being that's the offspring of a god and a human. Their power is usually greater than a mortal's but less than a god's.

GORGON: Three sisters (Medusa, Stheno, and Euryale) who had snakes for hair and whose gaze would turn people to stone.

GREECE: A country in Southeast Europe. Today, Athens is its capital.

ITHAKA: A Greek island in the Ionian Sea.

LOOM: A tool that makes fabric by weaving yarn or thread.

MEDDLE: To interfere in something that's not one's concern.

MORTAL: Someone who is able to die. What the gods and goddesses called humans.

MOUNT OLYMPUS: The highest mountain in Greece, which is home to the gods and goddesses.

NYMPH: Nature spirits that often appear in the form of young, beautiful women.

QUEST: A challenge often given to a hero. Often, it includes a test or difficult tasks.

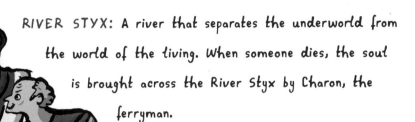

RIVER STYX: A river that separates the underworld from the world of the living. When someone dies, the soul is brought across the River Styx by Charon, the ferryman.

SIREN: A creature that is half woman, half bird who lures sailors to doom with her song.

SPARTA: A prominent Greek city that was one of the largest military powers.

SUITOR: Someone who pursues another person in the hopes of marriage.

TAPESTRY: A piece of fabric with pictures or design formed by weaving threads.

TEMPLE: A building for worshipping gods and goddesses.

TRIDENT: A three-pronged spear that's carried by Poseidon.

TROJAN HORSE: A large wooden horse that the Greeks used to sneak into Troy during the Trojan War.

TROJAN WAR: A war between Troy and Greece that began when Paris, the prince of Troy, eloped with Helen, the queen of Sparta.

TROY: A city in modern-day Turkey.

VANITY: Excessive pride in oneself or one's appearance.

WEAVE: To form fabric by interlacing threads at a right angle to each other.

SELECT BIBLIOGRAPHY

March, Jenny. *The Penguin Book of Classical Myths.* New York:
   Penguin, 2009.

Matyszak, Philip. *The Greek and Roman Myths: A Guide to the Classical
   Stories.* London: Thames & Hudson, 2010.

ABOUT THE AUTHOR

IMOGEN GREENBERG is a writer and podcaster who lives in London. She writes history and myths for children and is also the creator of Such Stuff, the podcast for Shakespeare's Globe.

ABOUT THE ILLUSTRATOR

ISABEL GREENBERG is an award-winning illustrator, comic artist, and writer. Her graphic novels The Encyclopedia of Early Earth and The One Hundred Nights of Hero are both New York Times bestsellers, and her latest graphic novel, Glass Town, was called a "lyrical, endlessly inventive book" by Publishers Weekly in a starred review. She is also the illustrator of four acclaimed nonfiction science books by author Seth Fishman. She lives in London and enjoys illustrating all things historical and fantastical.